This Little Tiger book belongs to:

_____

_____

_____

_____

For Sue and Paul
A.H.B.

For Jess
T.W.

LITTLE TIGER PRESS
An imprint of Magi Publications
1 The Coda Centre, 189 Munster Road,
London SW6 6AW, UK
www.littletigerpress.com
First published in Great Britain 1998
by Little Tiger Press, London
This edition published 2008
Printed in China
10 9 8 7 6 5 4 3 2 1

IT COULD HAVE BEEN WORSE

by **A.H. Benjamin**   Pictures by **Tim Warnes**

LITTLE TIGER PRESS

Mouse was on his way back home
after visiting his town cousin when . . .

WHOOPS!

he lost his
balance and fell
to the ground.

"Ouch!" said Mouse.
"This isn't my
lucky day."

But it could have
been worse!

Mouse picked himself up
and continued on his way.
He came to an open field
and was scurrying across it
when . . .

CRASH!

he fell into a dark hole.

"Why do things *always* go wrong for me?" grumbled Mouse.

But it could have been worse!

Mouse climbed out of the hole and
was off again, but soon he got sleepy.

"I think I'll take a rest," Mouse said.
He had just found a comfortable spot when . . .

OUCH!

he sat on a thistle
and shot into the air.

"Everything bad happens to me!" wailed Mouse as he pulled the thorns out of his fur.

But it could have been worse!

Mouse trotted down the hill until he reached a stream. He began to cross it using the stepping stones when . . .

"I'll catch a cold!"
complained Mouse.

But it could have been worse!

Mouse paddled to the edge of the
stream and climbed out of the water.

Shaking himself dry, he was just
about to scramble down a steep bank
when . . .

WHEEE!

he lost his footing and
skidded to the bottom.

"I'll be black and blue all over," cried Mouse.

But it could have been worse!

Mouse staggered to his feet and
ran the rest of the way home.

"It's been a terrible day," he said to his
mother as she bathed his cuts and bruises.
"I fell into a hole, got wet in the river, and—"
"Never mind, son," she said . . .

"It could have been much worse!"

fantastic reads from Little Tiger Press

BEWARE of the BEARS!
Alan MacDonald · Gwyneth Williamson

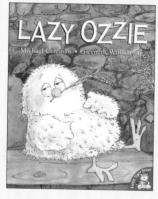

LAZY OZZIE
Michael Coleman · Gwynerie Williamson

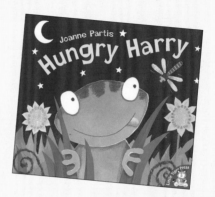

Joanne Partis
Hungry Harry

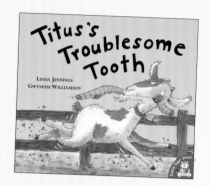

Titus's Troublesome Tooth
LINDA JENNINGS
Gwyneth Williamson

Little Tiger's big surprise!
Julie Sykes · Tim Warnes

Have you got my Purr?
Judy West
Tim Warnes

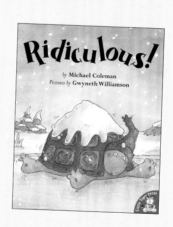

Ridiculous!
by Michael Coleman
Pictures by Gwyneth Williamson

Martin Hall and Catherine Walters
Charlie and Tess

For information regarding any of the above titles
or for our catalogue, please contact us:
Little Tiger Press, 1 The Coda Centre,
189 Munster Road, London SW6 6AW, UK
Tel: +44 (0)20 7385 6333 Fax: +44 (0)20 7385 7333
E-mail: info@littletiger.co.uk
www.littletigerpress.com

IT COULD HAVE BEEN WORSE
A.H. Benjamin · Tim Warnes

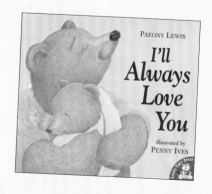

PAEONY LEWIS
I'll Always Love You
illustrated by
PENNY IVES